ICE AGE
DAWN OF THE DINOSAURS

MADE YOU LOOK!

Adapted by Nicole Congleton

HARPER

ENTERTAINMENT
An Imprint of HarperCollinsPublishers

HarperEntertainment is an imprint of HarperCollins Publishers.

Ice Age: Dawn of the Dinosaurs: Made You Look!
Ice Age: Dawn of the Dinosaurs ™ and © 2009 Twentieth Century Fox Film Corporation. All Rights Reserved.
Printed in the United States of America.

Library of Congress catalog card number: 2009922233
ISBN 978-0-06-169244-4
09 10 11 12 13 LP/WOR 10 9 8 7 6 5 4 3 2 1
Typography by Rick Farley
❖
First Edition

ARE YOU READY FOR SOME FUN?

The picture pairs in this book may seem the same,
but look closely—they're not! What's different?
Are there things missing?

Can you find all of the differences?

MADE YOU LOOK!

CAMPFIRE STORIES

Buck tells the gang about his first run-in with Rudy.

FOLLOW THE LEADER!

Sid leads his pack on a hike.

POSSUM POSSE

Ellie, Crash, and Eddie are like siblings.

MAMMAL PRIDE

Manny, Ellie, and Sid are furry and proud.

MOMMA MANIA

This dinosaur will fight for her little ones.

DID WE DO THAT?
Sid apologizes for the little dino's behavior.

MADE YOU LOOK
3
TIMES

HEY, WHAT'S THE BIG ACORN?

Scrat won't give up his favorite meal without a fight.

WHAT A VIEW!

Diego admires the beauty of the wild.

GOING UNDERGROUND

Ellie travels under the icy tundra to find Sid.

CHICKEN À LA WHAT?!

Sid isn't sure he likes his dinner plans.

SO SORRY

Sid and the dinos sure look guilty!

Scrat reaches out for his acorn in the snow.

MADE YOU LOOK
3
TIMES

EGG·STRA! EGG·STRA!

Suddenly, Sid has three mouths to feed.

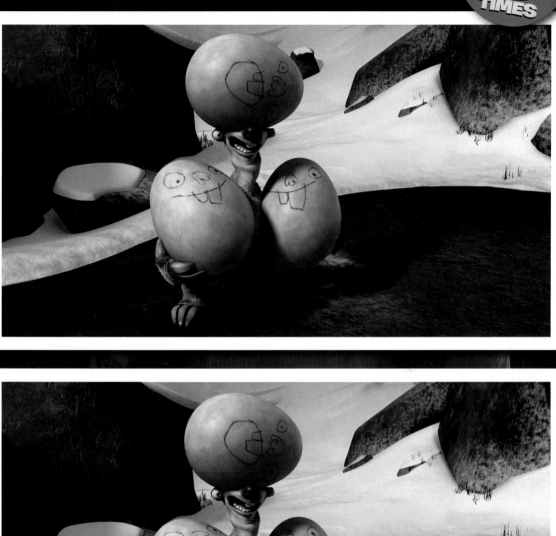

LUCKY WEASEL
Buck lives to tell the tale of Rudy.

HEARTWARMING

The ice mobile shows a loving family.

ACORN LOVE

Sparks fly between two rodents.

SAVE MY BABY!

One of Sid's eggs makes a fast roll-away.

MMM, LUNCH!
The dinosaurs eye their next meal.

NUTS!
This isn't an acorn!

ALL TOGETHER
Peaches meets her new uncles.

BONES

Momma sniffs a snack.

BUNGLE IN THE JUNGLE
There's no ice here!

PRIVACY, PLEASE!
What does it take for a squirrel to be alone?

MADE YOU LOOK
4
TIMES

TUNDRA TALK

Manny, Ellie, and Sid have a serious discussion.

Scrat holds on for his life.

AIR BUCK
This weasel travels in style!

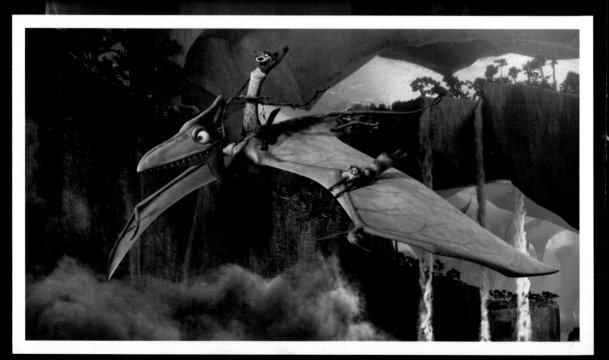

ANSWERS

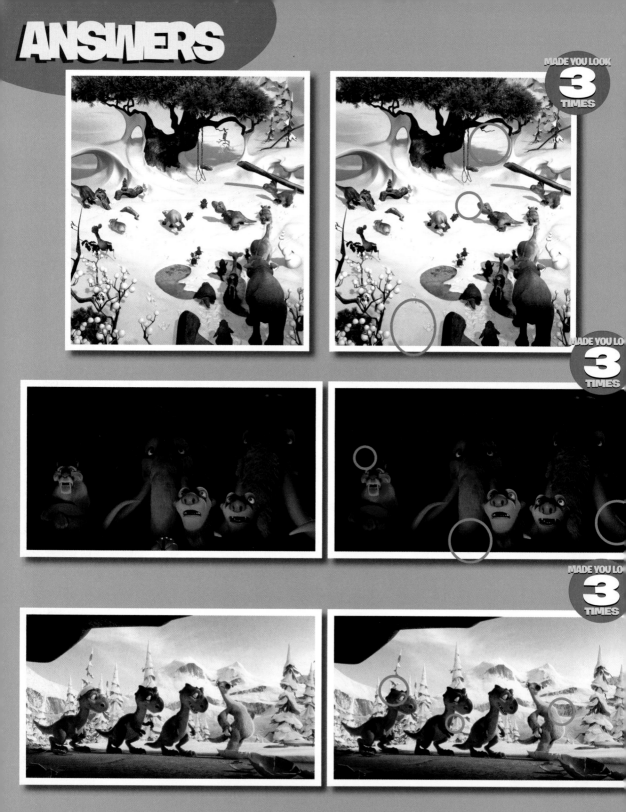

MADE YOU LOOK
3
TIMES

MADE YOU LOOK
3
TIMES

MADE YOU LOOK
3
TIMES

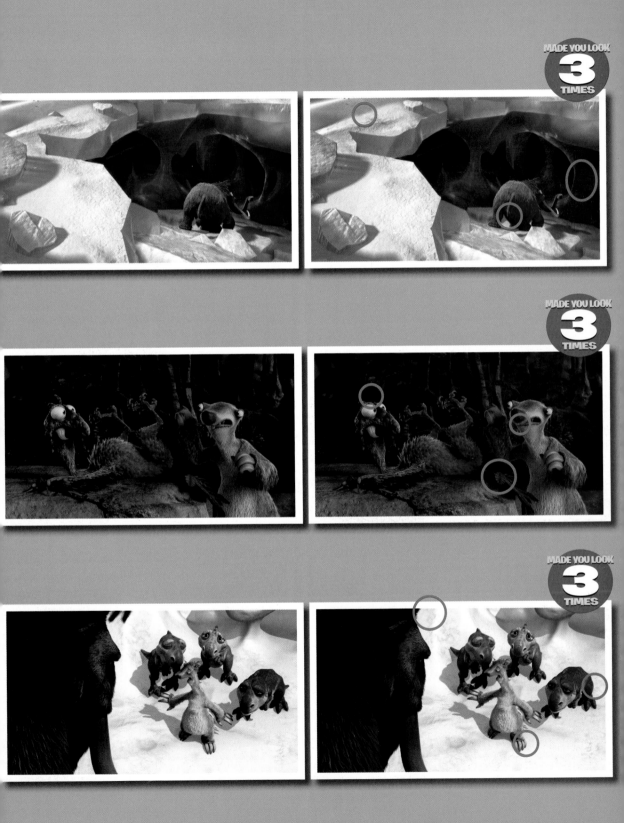

ANSWERS

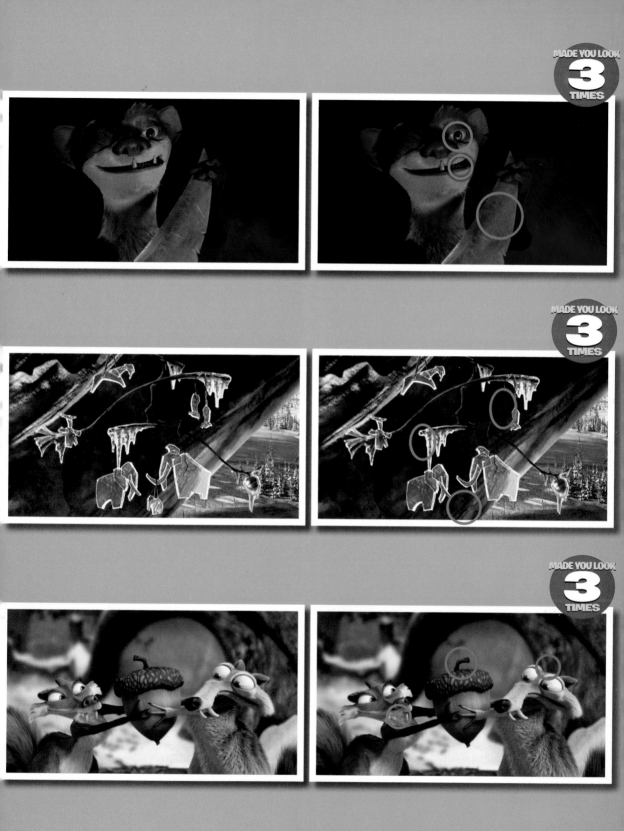

ANSWERS

ANSWERS